By Mary Man-Kong
Based on the original screenplay by Elise Allen
Illustrated by Rainmaker Entertainment

Special thanks to Rob Hudnut, Tiffany J. Shuttleworth, Vicki Jaeger and Monica Okazaki

A GOLDEN BOOK • NEW YORK

Published in the United States by Golden Books, an imprint of Random House Children's Books, a division of Random House, Inc., New York, and in Canada by Random House of Canada Limited, Toronto.
www.goldenbooks.com www.randomhouse.com/kids
Educators and librarians, for a variety of teaching tools, visit us at www.randomhouse.com/teachers
ISBN: 978-0-375-84427-0 Library of Congress Control Number: 2007940564
Printed in the United States of America 10 9 8 7 6 5 4 3 2

Bibble didn't know what to do. His puffball pal, Dizzle, had invited him for a visit. But Bibble wasn't sure he would fit in with all of Dizzle's friends. So Bibble decided to ask his friend Elina for advice.

"Let me tell you a story about a good friend of mine named Mariposa . . . ," said Elina.

Mariposa lived in a kingdom of beautiful butterfly fairies in a magical place called Flutterfield. But the butterfly fairies didn't like the dark, because that was when the hungry Skeezites came out.

Queen Marabella filled the trees with magical glowing flowers to keep the Skeezites away. As long as Marabella lived, Flutterfield was safe.

But Mariposa was different from all the other fairies. She liked the dark sky because she loved studying the stars. "Look," Mariposa said as she pointed out a constellation to her best friend, Willa. "There's the Archer's bow and arrow."

But Willa was scared of the dark. "We'd better get going before the Skeezites come out," she said.

Mariposa and Willa worked for two sisters named Rayna and Rayla.

"I have nothing to wear to the ball tonight!" said Rayna. "Mariposa, have all my gowns befluttered."

"And I need shiny thistleburst for my hair, Willa," demanded Rayla. "The prince is going to be at the ball, and we have to look perfect."

With their arms full of fairy dresses, Mariposa and Willa hurried to get the two sisters ready for the ball.

Later that day, Rayna, Rayla, and Willa eagerly arrived at the palace ball. But Mariposa didn't want to go inside, because she didn't think she'd fit in. She decided to stay outside and read a book.

Outside the palace, Mariposa saw Henna, the queen's royal assistant. Henna was very popular and fit in with any crowd.

"Are you coming to the ball?" asked Henna.

"No, I just don't think I'd have much fun," Mariposa explained. "But you wouldn't understand."

"Sometimes I don't feel as if I belong, either," said Henna as she flew toward the palace doors. "But I'll get to where I want to be."

Mariposa thought Henna was a very kind fairy—but Henna had a dark secret! She was plotting to poison the queen and take over Flutterfield!

As Mariposa flew around the palace reading her book, she bumped into Prince Carlos. He didn't like parties, either, and was reading the same book as Mariposa.

The prince was impressed by Mariposa's knowledge of the stars and her interest in faraway places.

Later that night, he asked Mariposa for her help.

"The queen is very sick," said the prince. "Without her, Flutterfield's lights will go out and we will all be in danger. Can you take this map and find the cure?"

Mariposa promised to help, but she wasn't sure she could do it on her own.

When Rayna and Rayla heard about Mariposa's secret mission for the prince, they volunteered to help.

"We will be the ones to save Flutterfield, win the queen's undying gratitude, and impress the prince!" said Rayla.

Mariposa, Rayna, and Rayla quickly set off on their journey. Soon the safety of Flutterfield's lights was far behind them—and Skeezites were everywhere! And to make matters worse, Rayna lost the map!

Mariposa remembered they needed to go east to a place called the Bewilderness. Using her knowledge of the stars, she located the Archer's arrow, which pointed east, and followed it.

In the Bewilderness, they met Zinzie the Meewah. Zinzie didn't know where the cure was, but she knew two beautiful mermaids who could help them.

The mermaids agreed to help only if the fairies brought them rare Conkle Shells in return. Mariposa, Rayna, Rayla, and Zinzie dove into the water and soon found the Conkle Shells—but woke the Sea Beast! Luckily, the fairies worked together and quickly escaped the monster.

"Head east and you will find the cure in the Cave of Reflection," the mermaids said as they disappeared with their precious shells.

The friends flew for hours and finally reached the Cave of Reflection. As they entered the cave, they met a tiny fairy called the Fairy Speck.

"Your journey will end in the star chamber," said the Fairy Speck. "The cure is hidden there behind a star. Only one of you may choose the correct star."

Mariposa didn't think she could do it, but Rayna and Rayla knew she was the bravest and smartest fairy for the job.

"I know the Archer is a navigator," Mariposa said as she looked up at a constellation. "His arrow will point to the correct star." But the arrow was pointing to one lone star that didn't fit in with the others. She wondered if that could be the correct star.

"Every star is there for a reason," said Mariposa. "They don't have to fit in to be important. They just have to be themselves. And that is the star I choose."

As Mariposa chose the lone star, she was swept into a magical whirlwind of light and colors. The star transformed into the cure—and Mariposa's wings magically grew larger and sparkled beautifully!

With the cure in hand, Mariposa and her friends raced to the palace to save the queen.

As the lights slowly went out in Flutterfield, Henna took control of the kingdom with her horrible Skeezites. Prince Carlos tried to hold off the Skeezites, but there were just too many of them.

Mariposa flew quickly through the palace and discovered Henna in the queen's chambers.

"You've never felt as if you belonged in Marabella's kingdom," Henna told Mariposa, trying to trick her. "But you will in mine. Everyone will love you."

"I'm happy with who I am," Mariposa declared as she flew to the queen's side with the cure. Queen Marabella awoke and Flutterfield shone brightly. The Skeezites quickly fled—along with the evil fairy, Henna. "This isn't over, Flutterfield!" Henna shrieked. "I'll be back!"

Flutterfield was saved!

Prince Carlos and Queen Marabella were very grateful and gave Mariposa, Rayna, Rayla, and Zinzie beautiful fairy headbands as a reward.

As Mariposa flew away with her fairy friends, she realized she was special just as she was.

"So you see, Bibble," Elina said, "the most beautiful thing you can be is yourself."

Just then, Dizzle appeared. "Ready to go, Bibble?"

Bibble looked at Elina and smiled. "You bet!" he said. He wasn't afraid of not fitting in anymore. He knew he was special just as he was.